Wubbzy Gets Lost

Adapted by Lauren Cecil
Based on an episode by Frederick Stroppel

ISBN 978-0-545-26498-3

Based on the TV series Wow! Wow! Wubbzy! as seen on Nick Jr.® created by
Bob Boyle.

Published by Scholastic Inc. SCHOLASTIC and associated logos are trademarks and/or
registered trademarks of Scholastic Inc.

12 11 10 9 8 7 6 5 4 3 2 1   10 11 12 13 14 15/0

Printed in China. First printing, September 2010

SCHOLAST!C INC.
New York   Toronto   London   Auckland   Sydney
Mexico City   New Delhi   Hong Kong

Wubbzy, Walden, and Widget were going camping.
"I love camping!" Wubbzy said. "I can't wait to catch some flying frogs at the pond!"

When they arrived at their campsite,
Wubbzy was ready to head straight to the pond.
"Let's go!" Wubbzy cried.

"Wait!" Widget called. "First we have to unload the truck."

"Then we have to unpack the bags," Walden said.

"And *then* we have to pitch the tent," Widget added.

"But that's going to take *forever*!" Wubbzy wailed.
"Not if we all work as a team!" Widget said.

The frog led Wubbzy right to the pond.
"Walden! Widget!" Wubbzy shouted. "Boy am I glad to see you!"
"We're glad to see you too!" Walden said.
"Did you get lost, Wubbster?" Widget asked.

"Just a little," Wubbzy admitted. "I should have waited for you. And I shouldn't have gone off by myself."

"At least now you can catch some flying frogs!" Walden said.
Wubbzy thought for a moment.
"No thanks," he said. "Those frogs need to be free, so they can help others who get lost."

"It's getting dark," Wubbzy said. "Which way back to the camp?" asked Walden, looking for the map.

"I'm not sure," Widget said.

"Uh-oh!" said Wubbzy.

Then the frog hopped in front of them.
He could show them the way back to camp.
"Follow that frog!" Wubbzy said.
"Wow, wow, RIBBIT!"